Animals That Help Us

Military Animals

by Wiley Blevins

LOOK! BOOKS™

Red Chair Press   Egremont, Massachusetts

Look! Books are produced and published by Red Chair Press:
Red Chair Press LLC   PO Box 333   South Egremont, MA 01258-0333
www.redchairpress.com

Publisher's Cataloging-In-Publication Data

Names: Blevins, Wiley

Title: Military animals / by Wiley Blevins.

Description: Egremont, Massachusetts : Red Chair Press, [2018] | Series: Look! books : Animals that help us | Interest age level: 004-007. | Includes Now You Know fact-boxes, a glossary, and resources for additional reading. | Includes index. | Summary: "You know that pets can be fun. But some dogs, horses, pigs, and more have important jobs to do. With Animals That Help Us young readers will discover how animals help us stay safe. With Military Animals, readers discover common and uncommon helpers from dogs and horses to dolphins, bees, elephants, and more."-- Provided by publisher.

Identifiers: ISBN 978-1-63440-317-7 (library hardcover) | ISBN 978-1-63440-365-8 (paperback) | ISBN 978-1-63440-323-8 (ebook)

Subjects: LCSH: Animals--War use--Juvenile literature. | Animals in police work--Juvenile literature. | CYAC: Animals--War use. | Working animals.

Classification: LCC UH87 .B54 2018 (print) | LCC UH87 (ebook) | DDC 355.4/24 [E]--dc23

LCCN 2017947559

Copyright © 2019 Red Chair Press LLC
RED CHAIR PRESS, the RED CHAIR and associated logos are registered trademarks of Red Chair Press LLC.

All rights reserved. No part of this book may be reproduced, stored in an information or retrieval system, or transmitted in any form by any means, electronic, mechanical including photocopying, recording, or otherwise without the prior written permission from the Publisher. For permissions, contact info@redchairpress.com

Photo credits: Shutterstock except for the following; p. 7: © Xavier ROSSI/Getty Images; p. 9: © INDRANIL MUKHERJEE/Getty Images; p. 13: © Getty Images

Printed in the United States of America

0718 1P CGF18

Table of Contents

Animals on Land 4
Animals in the Water 12
Animals in the Air 16
Words to Keep 23
Learn More at the Library 23
Index 24

Animals on Land

DOGS Dogs are man's best friend. They can bark to warn **soldiers** of danger. They can bite or attack an **enemy**. They can also look for people in damaged buildings. Dogs to the **rescue**!

Dogs help search for people trapped after an earthquake.

5

RATS Most people don't want rats at home. But they are welcome on battlefields. Large African rats can smell very well. They have been **trained** to find land mines and bombs.

Good to Know

The large rats stick their nose high in the air when they smell TNT used in land mines and bombs.

land mine

Rats help people clear fields of old land mines. This saves lives!

7

HORSES Horses are fast and strong. They can carry heavy loads. Many years ago, before tanks, soldiers rode horses into battle. Today, horses are used to get to places tanks can't go.

These soldiers are training horses to carry heavy weapons.

9

ELEPHANTS Long ago, people used elephants in war. Elephants could carry heavy loads. They could also crush an enemy. But one thing always stopped them. Pigs. Elephants are scared of their squeals.

Elephants used in battles are honored in Thailand and India.

Animals in the Water

DOLPHINS Dolphins are very smart and loyal. They can find mines under the water. These mines can blow up a ship. Cameras help humans see what the dolphin finds under water. Dolphins help keep ships safe.

camera

13

SEA LIONS Sea lions have great sight. They have been trained to spot underwater bombs. They can also swim fast. Sea lions can sneak up on an enemy swimmer or spy near a boat and trap him.

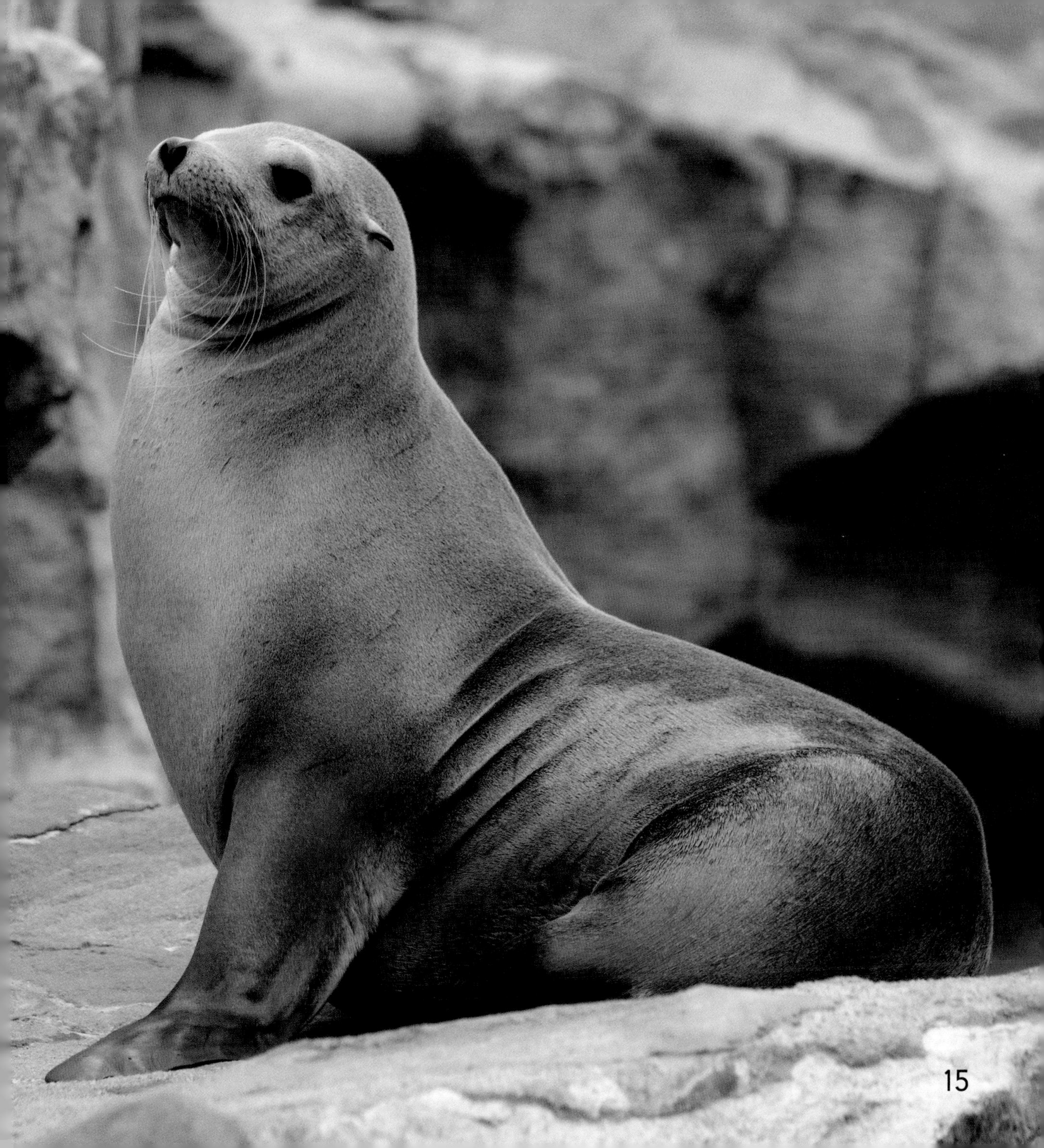

Animals in the Air

PIGEONS Pigeons have been used to send top-secret news during war. Soldiers put a note on the pigeon's leg. The pigeon flies through the battle. The secret note safely gets to the right person. And fast!

Good to Know

Pigeons always fly home. So the birds had to be sent from one place to another first—by train or by troops in war. Then the pigeons would return home with secret notes from the front lines.

BATS Not all flying animals are easy to train. People have tried to use bats in war. They trained the bats to drop tiny bombs in buildings. But the bats flew wherever they wanted. *Oops!*

19

BEES No one likes to get stung by a bee. So, long ago beehives were thrown into enemy camps. *Ouch!*

Today, bees are being trained to sniff out bombs. Bees have a very good sense of smell.

ROBO BUGS Not all **military** animals bark, bite, or sting. Robo bugs, called drones, are being made by scientists. These flying robots have cameras in them. They might be the military animals of the future!

Words to Keep

enemy: a person (or country) who is against you
military: related to soldiers or the army
rescue: to save
soldier: a person who fights in a war
train: to teach

Learn More at the Library

Books (Check out these books to learn more.)

Gabe: The Dog Who Sniffs Out Danger (Ready-to-Read) by Thea Feldman. Simon Spotlight, 2014.

Military Animals by Laurie Calkhoven. Scholastic, 2015.

Pigeon Hero (Ready-to-Read) by Shirley Raye Redman. Simon Spotlight, 2003.

Web Sites (Ask an adult to show you this web site.)

Animal Planet: Military Animals
http://www.animalplanet.com/tv-shows/saved/photos/military-animals-pictures/

Index

Bats 18

Bees 20

Dogs 4

Dolphins 12

Elephants 10

Horses 8

Pigeons 16

Rats 6

Robo Bugs 22

Sea Lions 14

About the Author

Wiley Blevins has never been in the military, but he was on the front lines in the classroom for many years.